THIS WALKER BOOK BELONGS TO:

_____

_____

_____

_____

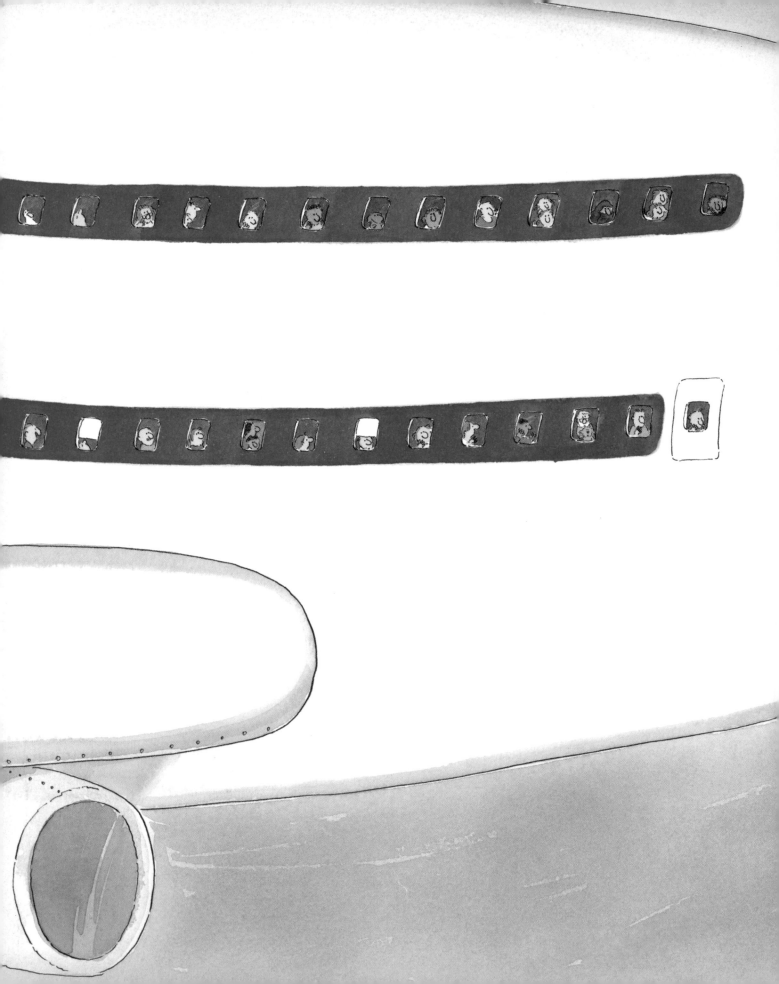

For Wendy,
my editor and friend

First published 2000 by Walker Books Ltd
87 Vauxhall Walk, London SE11 5HJ

This edition published 2001

2 4 6 8 10 9 7 5 3 1

© 2000 Bob Graham

The characters in this book have
appeared in the magazine Pomme D'Api,
published by Bayard Presse, France, in 1997

This book has been typeset in Stempel Schneidler Medium

Printed in Hong Kong

British Library Cataloguing in Publication Data:
a catalogue record for this book
is available from the British Library

ISBN 0-7445-8905-3

WALKER BOOKS
AND SUBSIDIARIES
LONDON • BOSTON • SYDNEY

MAX

Bob Graham

Morning arrived on a
street like any other street,
in a town like any other town.

In a house the colour of
the sun and the shape
of a lightning bolt, a baby
woke in his cot.

Not just any baby.
He was a superbaby –
son of superheroes,
Captain Lightning and
Madam Thunderbolt.

Imagine him behind those
yellow walls, his fingers
curling and his feet kicking.

His name was …

Max.

His parents – legendary catchers of thieves and bullies –
loved Max dearly.

"You can walk already,"
said Max's dad,

"and you can
talk already,

and I think that
you'll soon be …

flying like a bird!"

"He'll be a superhero, just like us!" said his grandma.

"But first he'll need to fly!" said his grandad.

Although they bounced him and bumped him, and threw him like a feather on the wind ...

Max did not fly. He just floated
gently back to earth.

Max grew, as superbabies do. But still he didn't fly.

"Just hover a little," said Madam Thunderbolt,

"every superhero needs to hover and hurtle and swoop."

"Well, maybe sometime soon," she added.

At home, Max and Phantom the dog played on the floor.

"Come on up and join me with the budgie!" said his dad.

"I can't," said Max. "I want to play with Phantom."

"He walked and talked so early," said Captain Lightning, "I can't understand why he doesn't fly."

"When I was his age," said his grandad, "I got into trouble for leaving fingermarks on the lampshade."

By the time he went to school,
Max was not a flying superhero,
but just an ordinary boy with
a cape and a mask …

which were no help to him at all in the school yard.

"Why don't you do tough things like your mum and dad?

And why do you dress in those funny clothes?" said Aaron.

"Why don't you fly?" asked Daisy.

Max just shrugged.

The sun rose one morning with the world famous superheroes
deep in dreams of yesterday's exploits.

Grandma and Grandad dreamed of heroic past deeds.
Phantom dreamed of rabbits.

Who could know that
a baby bird was about
to fall from its nest?

Max knew.
Max saw it from
his open window.
This bird was
not ready to fly.

He ran to the stairs,

and took
them three
at a time.

He reached
the front door,

and pulled
it open.

The baby bird fell.
Max flew to save it.

PLOP!

Max flew the baby bird back to its nest.
"You be careful up there, Max," called Captain Lightning.
Madam Thunderbolt swelled with pride.

In the weeks that followed, Max could be seen hovering
like a summer dragonfly above the school gates.

Try as she might, Miss Honeyset couldn't keep
him firmly in his seat in class.

At lunchtime in the school yard,
to his friends he was still
plain and ordinary "Max"...

Well, not *quite* ordinary.
But then as Aaron said,
"Everyone's different
in *some* way, aren't they?"

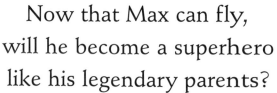

Now that Max can fly,
will he become a superhero
like his legendary parents?

Will he hurtle and swoop
to catch thieves, crooks
and bullies?

"Not important," said Madam Thunderbolt.
"Let's call him a small hero; a small hero doing quiet deeds.
The world needs more of those."

Max wished his mum wouldn't hug him in public.

Now on Sundays, after their week's work is finished,
Captain Lightning, Madam Thunderbolt and Max
ride high in the warm air over the town.

"Can we go up into the jet-stream?" asks Max.
"Whenever you're ready, Max," answer the legendary
superheroes, Captain Lightning and Madam Thunderbolt.

BOB GRAHAM says that **Max**, Gold Award Winner of the Smarties Book Prize, presented a special challenge to him. "In previous books I tried to make the ordinary extraordinary, but here my problem was just the opposite: how to make this extraordinary family seem *ordinary*!"

Bob is Australia's leading picture book maker, although he has been living in England for many years. He has written and illustrated numerous titles for Walker Books, including *Has Anyone Here Seen William?*; *Grandad's Magic*; *Brand New Baby*; *Rose Meets Mr Wintergarten*; *Queenie the Bantam* (Highly Commended for the Kate Greenaway Medal); *Buffy* (Smarties Book Prize Silver Award Winner); and *Let's Get a Pup*. He also illustrated *This Is Our House*, written by Michael Rosen.

Bob is married with two grown-up children and lives in Somerset.

ISBN 0-7445-6970-2 (pb)

ISBN 0-7445-7807-8 (pb)

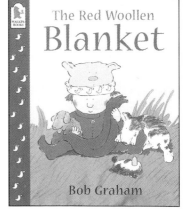

ISBN 0-7445-7808-6 (pb)